Hector and Hummingbird

Nicholas John Frith

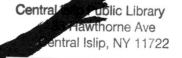

ARTHUR A. LEVINE BOOKS
AN IMPRINT OF SCHOLASTIC INC.

Deep in the mountains of Peru lived a bear called Hector and a hummingbird called Hummingbird. They were the best of friends.

Mostly.

But sometimes,
Hector got cross
with Hummingbird.

Whenever Hector just wanted
a nice, quiet snack,

Hummingbird wouldn't stop talking . . .

Hey, Hector!
Is that a custard apple?

I love custard apples!
I'm going to eat this one!
Oh, no! I'm going to eat that one!

Shall I eat your one?
Hector?
Hec-torrr!

And whenever Hector wanted a nice, quiet scratch on a tree,

Hummingbird wouldn't stop copying him . . .

Hey, Hector!
Are you scratching?
I'm going to scratch too!

And whenever Hector just wanted a nice, quiet nap in the branches, Hummingbird wouldn't leave him alone . . .

Hey, Hector!

Are you asleep? Shall I sleep too?

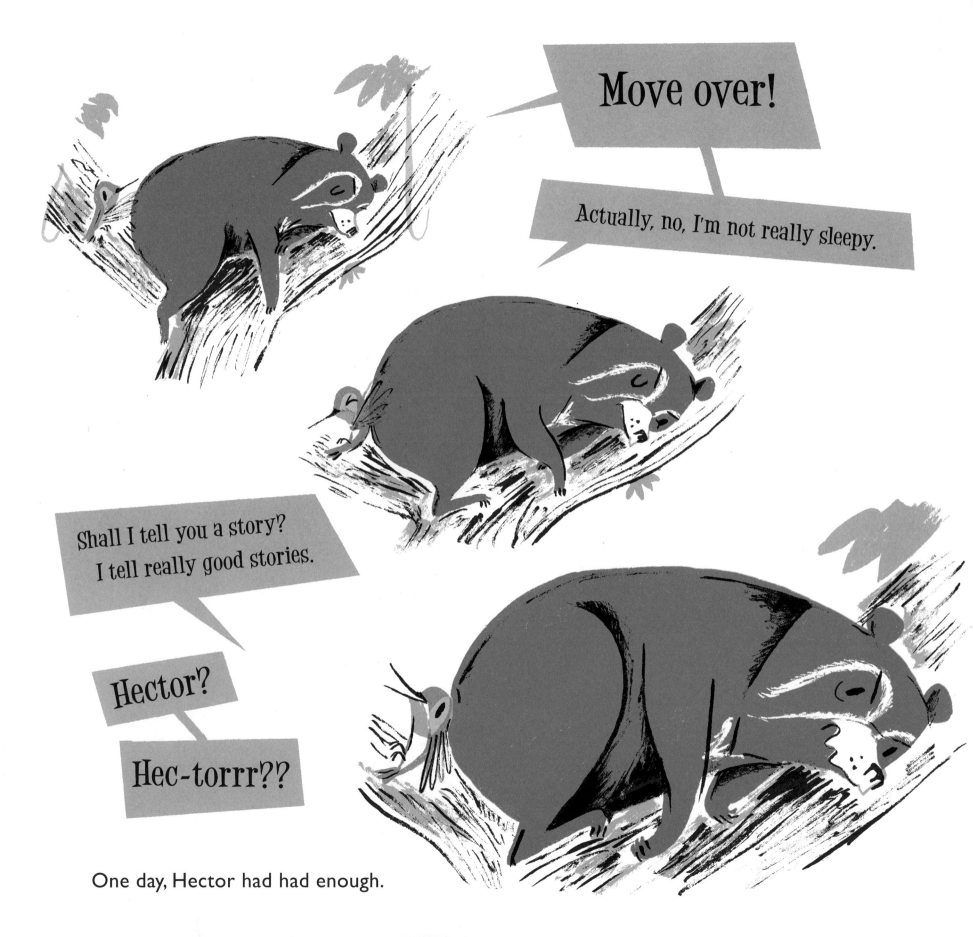

One day, Hector had had enough.

"ARRGH!!"

cried Hector.

"Leave me alone!"

Hector stomped off into the jungle.
"I'm going to find a bit of peace and quiet!"

Hummingbird was sad. He'd never known
Hector was cross with him.

He decided he'd better follow and find out why.

Hey, Hector!

What's peace and quiet?

Is it in the jungle?
Can I help look for it?

"Stop following me!" said Hector.
"I want to be on my own!"

So Hummingbird
stopped following him.

Mostly.

Hector walked deep into the jungle.

At last he was on his own. He felt very excited.

But a little bit odd.

Maybe he was
just hungry.

So Hector picked a custard apple,
and sat down to have a nice, quiet snack.

The fruit was sweet.
And delicious.

But it felt funny eating it on his own. "Hummingbird would really like this custard apple," thought Hector.

Next Hector found what looked like the scratchiest tree in the jungle. He settled down to have a nice, quiet scratch.

But it felt funny scratching on his own.

"Hummingbird would love
scratching on this tree,"
sighed Hector.

SQUAWK!

Dark fell, and Hector settled down for a nap.
The jungle was noisy at night, and a little bit scary.
Hector couldn't sleep.

AARK!

SQUEAK!

EEK!

"I wish Hummingbird were here,"
sniffed Hector. "He could
tell me a story."

"Hummingbird!" cried Hector.
"You're here! I missed you!"

I missed you too!

Except I was here all along.

"Here all along?" said Hector.
"I thought I told you not to follow me!"

But why?

"Because you never stop talking!"

I'm just being friendly.

"And you're always copying me!"

You always have really good ideas.

"Oh," said Hector. "Really?"

Just then, Hector had his best idea yet.

"Hummingbird, can you copy me now,
by being really, really quiet?"

And he did.
Mostly.

Hey, Hector?

This is fun, isn't it?

We're being really, really quiet, aren't we?

I love being quiet, don't you?

Hector? Hec-torrr?

How many of these animals did you spot in the jungle?

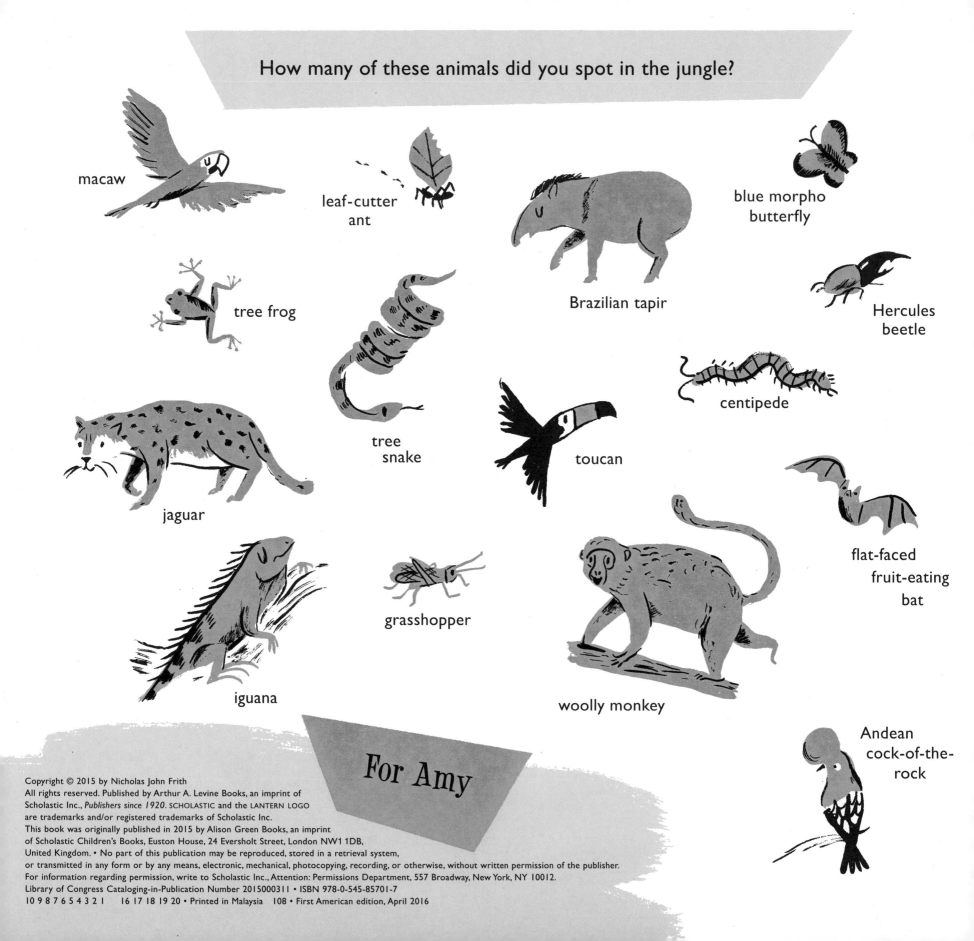

macaw

leaf-cutter ant

Brazilian tapir

blue morpho butterfly

tree frog

Hercules beetle

tree snake

centipede

jaguar

toucan

flat-faced fruit-eating bat

iguana

grasshopper

woolly monkey

Andean cock-of-the-rock

For Amy

This book was originally published in 2015 by Alison Green Books, an imprint
of Scholastic Children's Books, Euston House, 24 Eversholt Street, London NW1 1DB,
United Kingdom. • No part of this publication may be reproduced, stored in a retrieval system,
or transmitted in any form or by any means, electronic, mechanical, photocopying, recording, or otherwise, without written permission of the publisher.
For information regarding permission, write to Scholastic Inc., Attention: Permissions Department, 557 Broadway, New York, NY 10012.
Library of Congress Cataloging-in-Publication Number 2015000311 • ISBN 978-0-545-85701-7
10 9 8 7 6 5 4 3 2 1   16 17 18 19 20 • Printed in Malaysia   108 • First American edition, April 2016